The Cat and the Mouse
A Book of Persian
Fairy Tales

Hartwell James

The Cat and the Mouse: A Book of Persian Fairy Tales

Contact:
BibliotechPress@gmail.com

The present edition is a reproduction of 1906 publication of this work. Minor typographical errors may have been corrected without note, however, for an authentic reading experience the spelling, punctuation, and capitalization have been retained from the original text.

ISBN: 978-1-61895-098-7

Contents

Introduction

Persia is rich in folk lore. For hundreds and hundreds of years the stories in this book, and many others as well, have been told to the wondering boys and girls of that country, who, as they hear them, picture their native land as one of roses and tulips, where beautiful fairies build their castles in the rosy morn, and black gnomes fly around in the darkness of midnight.

A land, too, where the sun gleams like a fire above the blue mountains, and the water lilies are mirrored in the deep lakes. A land where the eyes of the tigers gleam through the reeds by the riverside, and dark-eyed, sunburned people are quick to love and quick to hate.

The belief in the "Ghool," or "Old Man of the Desert," is still prevalent in Persia, which probably accounts for the popularity of the story of "The Son of the Soap Seller." The other stories selected for this volume are great favorites, but the story of "The Cat and the Mouse" is perhaps the most popular of all.

The frontispiece to this volume is a reduced facsimile of a whole page in a Persian book, showing both the pictures and the reading as they were published in Persia. The other illustrations for "The Cat and the Mouse" are copies of drawings by a Persian artist.

"Two friends on one carpet may with contentment sleep;
Two monarchs in one kingdom the peace can never keep.
While earth revolves, and little children play,
Cats over mice will always hold the sway."

H. J.

THE CAT AND THE MOUSE

Showing how one may be lost in wonder at the story
of the cat and the mouse, when related with a
clear and rolling voice, as if from a pulpit.

ACCORDING to the decree of Heaven, there once
lived in the Persian city of Kerman a cat like
unto a dragon—a longsighted cat who hunted like

a lion; a cat with fascinating eyes and long whiskers and sharp teeth. Its body was like a drum, its beautiful fur like ermine skin.

Nobody was happier than this cat, neither the newly-wedded bride, nor the hospitable master of the house when he looks round on the smiling faces of his guests.

This cat moved in the midst of friends, boon companions of the saucepan, the cup, and the milk jug of the court, and of the dinner table when the cloth is spread.

Perceiving the wine cellar open, one day, the cat ran gleefully into it to see if he could catch a mouse, and hid himself behind a wine jar. At that moment a mouse ran out of a hole in the wall, quickly climbed the jar, and putting his head into it, drank so long and so deeply that he became drunk, talked very stupidly, and fancied he was as bold as a lion.

"Where is the cat?" shouted he, "that I may off with his head. I would cut off his head as if on the battlefield. A cat in front of me would fare worse than any dog who might happen to cross my path."

The cat ground his teeth with rage while hearing this. Quicker than the eye could follow, he made a spring, seized the mouse in his claws, and said, "Oh, little mouse, now will you take off my head?"

"I am thy servant," replied the mouse; "forgive my sin. I was drunk. I am thy slave; a slave whose ear is pierced and on whose shoulder the yoke is."

"Tell fewer lies," replied the cat. "Was there ever such a liar? I heard all you said and you shall pay for your sin with your life. I will make your life less than that of a dead dog."

So the cat killed and ate the mouse; but afterwards, being sorry for what he had done, he ran to the Mosque, and passed his hands over his face, poured water on his hands, and anointed himself as he had seen the faithful do at the appointed hours of prayer.

Then he began to recite the beautiful chapter to Allah in the Holy Book of the Persians, and to make his confession in this wise:

"I have repented, and will not again tear the body of a mouse with my teeth. I will give bread to the deserving poor. Forgive my sin, O great Forgiver, for have I not come to Thee bowed down with sorrow?"

He repeated this so many times and with so much feeling that he really thought he meant it, and finally wept for grief.

A little mouse happened to be behind the pulpit, and overhearing the cat's vows, speedily carried the glad but surprising news to the other mice. Breathlessly he related how that the cat had become a true Mussulman; how that he had seen him in the Mosque weeping and lamenting, and saying:

"Oh, Creator of the world, put away my sin, for I have offended like a big fool." Then the mouse went on to describe how that the cat had a rosary of beads, and made pious reflections in the spirit of a true penitent.

The mice began to make merry when they heard this startling news, for they were exceedingly glad. Seven chosen mice, each the headman of the village, arose and gave thanks that the cat should at last have entered the fold of the true believers.

All danced and shouted, "Ah! Ah! Hu! Hu!" and drank red wine and white wine until they were very merry. Two rang bells, two played castanets, and two sang. One carried a tray behind his back laden with good things, so that all could help themselves; some smoked water-pipes; another acted like a clown; others played various tunes on different instruments of music.

A few days after the feast, the King of the mice said to them, "Oh, friends, all of you bring costly presents worthy of the cat!" Then the mice scattered in search of gifts, but soon returned, each bearing something worthy of presentation, even to a nobleman.

One brought a bottle of wine; another a dish full of raisins; others came with salted nuts and melon seeds, lumps of cheese, basins of sugar-candy, pistachio nuts, little cakes iced with sugar, bottles of lemon juice, Indian shawls, hats, cloaks and many other things.

Discreetly they bore their gifts before the King of the Cats. When in the royal presence, they made humble obeisances, touching their foreheads on the ground, and saluting him, said:

"Oh, master, liberator of the lives of all, we have brought gifts worthy of thy service. We beseech thee to deign to accept of them."

Then the cat thought to himself, "I am rewarded for becoming a pious Mussulman. Though I have endured much hunger, yet this day finds me freely and amply provided for. Not for many days have I broken my fast. It is clear that Allah is appeased."

Then he turned to the mice, and bade them come nearer, calling them his friends. And they went forward trembling. So frightened were they that they were hardly aware of what they were doing. When they were close the cat made a sudden spring upon them.

Five mice he caught, each one the chief of a village; two with his front paws, two with his hind ones, and one in his mouth. The remaining mice barely escaped with their lives.

Picking up one of their murdered brothers, they quickly carried the sad news to the mice, saying: "Why do ye sit still, oh mice? Throw dust on your heads, oh young men, for the cruel cat has seized five of our unsuspecting companions with teeth and claws and has killed them."

Then for the space of five days they rent their clothes as do the mourners, and cast dust on their heads. Then they said: "We must go and tell our King all that has befallen the mice. We must not fail to tell him this calamity."

Whereupon they all rose up and went their way in deep sorrow; one beating the muffled drum, one tolling the bell; all had shawls around their necks; their tears the while running in little streams down their whiskers.

Arrived where the King was sitting on his throne, the mice paid homage to him, saying: "Master, we are subjects and thou art King. Behold the cat has treated us cruelly since he became a pious follower of Mahomet. Whereas, before his conversion he was wont to catch only one of us in a year, now that he is a sincere Mussulman his appetite has so increased that only five at a time will satisfy him."

Whereupon the King fell into such a violent rage that he resembled a saucepan boiling over. But to the deputation of mice he spoke very kindly, calling them his newly-arrived and welcome guests, and to comfort them vowed that he would give the cat such a chastisement that the news of it should circulate through the world.

Then, observing their grief, he commanded that the dead mouse should be buried with all pomp and ceremony. Accordingly they made lamentation for a whole week, as though it had been for one of royal degree; and having prepared delicious sweetmeats, they placed them in baskets and carried them with streaming eyes to the grave.

After the burial service, the King ordered the army to assemble on a given day on the great sandy plain that stretches as far as the eye can see around the city. Then he addressed them, saying:

"Oh, men and soldiers, inasmuch as the cat has so cruelly ill-treated our countrymen, he being a heretic and an evil doer, and brutal in nature, we must now go to the city of Kerman and fight him."

So three hundred and thirty thousand mice went forth, armed with swords, guns, and spears; and with flags and pennons bravely flying. A passing Arab from the desert, skilfully balancing himself on the back of a swift-traveling camel by means of a long pole, spied the great army in motion, and was so overcome with astonishment that he lost his balance and fell off. Several regiments of mice were put out of action by his fall; but nothing daunted, the army pressed on.

When the army was ready for battle, the King again addressed them saying: "O young men, an ambassador must be sent to the cat, one who is able, discreet, and eloquent." Then they all shouted: "The King's orders shall be carried out! Upon our heads be it."

Now, there was present a learned and eloquent mouse, the ruler of a province, and he it was that the King commanded to go as an ambassador to the cat in the city of Kerman. Almost before his name was out of the King's mouth, he had jumped out of his place in the ranks, and, traveling swiftly as the winds of the desert, he went in boldly before the cat and said:

"As an ambassador from the King of the Mice am I come, bowed down with grief and fatigue. Know this, my master has determined to wage war, and is even now come with his army to take off your head."

The cat roared out in reply, "Go tell your King to eat dust! I come not out of this city except at my good pleasure!" Then he sent messengers to bring up quickly some fighting and hunting cats from Khorassan—the land of the sun—to Kerman.

As soon as the cat's army was ready, the King of the Cats gave them marching orders, promising to come himself to the battle on the next day. The cats came out on horseback, each one like a hungry tiger. The mice also mounted their steeds, armed to the teeth, and boiling with rage. Shouting "Allah! Allah!" the armies fell upon each other with unsheathed swords.

So many cats and mice were killed that there was no room for the horses' feet. The cats fought valiantly, their fierce attacks carrying them through the first line of the mice, then through the second, and many Ameers and chiefs were killed. The mice, thinking the battle lost, turned to flee, crying out:

"Throw dust upon your heads, young men!"

But afterwards, rallying again, they faced their pursuers and attacked the right wing of the cat's army, shouting their battle cry of "Allah! Allah!"

In the thickest of the fray a mounted mouse speared the King of the Cats, so that he fell fainting to the ground. Before he could rise, the mouse leaped upon him and brought him captive to the King. So the cats were defeated on that day and sullenly retreated to the city of Kerman.

Having bound the cat, the mice beat him until he became unconscious. Then the plain echoed with the beating of tom-toms and shouts of joy. Then the King of the Mice seated himself on his throne and ordered the cat to be brought before him.

"Scoundrel!" he said to him, "Why hast thou eaten up my army? Hear now the King of the Mice." The cat hung his head in fear, and remained silent. After a few minutes, he said: "I am thy servant, even to death." Then the King replied:

"Carry this black-faced dog to the execution ground. I will come in person without delay to kill him in revenge for the blood of my slaughtered subjects."

So he mounted his elephant, and his guard marched proudly before him. The cat, with his hands tied together, stood weeping. Upon arriving at the execution grounds and discerning that the cat was not yet executed, the King said angrily to the hangman: "Why is it this prisoner is still alive? Hang him immediately!"

At that very moment a horseman came galloping furiously from the city and besought the King, saying: "Forgive this miserable cat; in future he will do us no harm." However, the King turned a deaf ear to his entreaties, ordering that the cat be killed at once. The mice hesitated, being unwilling, through fear, to carry out the order.

Of course, this made the King very angry. "O foolish mice!" he cried, "Ye will all take pity on the cat, in order that he may again make a sacrifice of you."

Directly the cat saw the horseman, his courage revived. With one bound he sprang from his place as does the tiger on his prey, burst his bonds asunder, and seized five unfortunate mice. The other mice, filled with dismay and terror, ran hither and thither, crying wildly:

"Allah! Allah! Shoot him! Cut off his head, as did Rastam his enemies on the day of battle!"

When the King of the Mice saw what, had happened, he fainted; whereupon the cat leaped on him, pulled off his crown, and placing the rope over his head, hanged him, so that he died immediately.

Then he darted here and there, seizing and slaying, and dashing mice to the earth, till the whole army of mice was routed, and there was none left to oppose him.

THE SON OF THE
SOAP SELLER

Cleverly proving that a princess with a necklace can frustrate the intentions of a Ghool, and that every king should have near his person the owner of a crystal cup.

THERE once dwelt a poor but worthy man named Abdullah in Meshed, the Holy City, the place of pilgrimage, whose beautiful mosque with the golden dome is the glory of the kingdom of Persia. He barely managed to get a living by the sale of soap.

All day long, from sunrise to sunset, he tramped the city, crying out: "O brothers, buy my pure soap. There is none better in the city, as every one knows. Even the little babes would say so if they could but speak."

Still, if you looked closely at it, you would never guess it to be soap; it was black and coarse, and more like wood than anything else. If any unlucky pilgrim used it on his face or hands, it would make his skin burn like fire. But this did not often happen, for the people in Persia do not use much soap on themselves, or their clothes, and sand does very well for cleaning cooking pots and pans. So it was that there were many days when poor Abdullah did not sell enough to buy sufficient bread for himself and his little boy Ahmed.

At such times, the father would creep sadly into his wretched mud- built hovel, and bury his face in his hands, so that he might not see his son trying to keep back the tears caused by hunger. The little fellow, however, now ten years of age, would comfort his father by saying:

"Inshallah"—if God wills—"to-morrow you will sell more soap than you have done for weeks past." And the father, looking into the bright, open face of his boy, would take courage, and pray that this might be so.

But the days went on and things became blacker and blacker, when one day an adventure befell little Ahmed. He was on his way to school, and as the sun was very hot, he sought the shelter of the big plane-trees that lined the banks of the stream flowing down the center of the principal street.

Women were filling their water jugs, or washing clothes; a string of camels were drinking; several donkeys were rolling playfully over and over in the water, and some dyers were wringing out newly-dyed garments, causing waves of many colors to flow past.

Just as Ahmed had stopped to look, a dervish, leading a fine lion by a chain, and some runners with curious hats and coats rushed past, shouting:

"Make way for the King! Turn your faces to the wall!" And there was the great King, seated on a beautiful Arabian horse, surrounded by soldiers. Then there passed a palanquin borne on the backs of four mules.

The party stopped just opposite to Ahmed, and from the palanquin there alighted a lady closely veiled, evidently wishing to inspect some beautiful Meshed silver work. Before she could reach the shop, a great tumult arose among the people. The lion had broken his chain and was madly leaping here and there, tearing and rending and dashing people to the ground. Women fainted, men fled, little children stood still and cried pitifully, some jumped into the stream; the frightened horses dashed madly through the crowd. All was terror and confusion.

Then with a roar the lion sprang upon the princess, and bore her to the ground; but ere he could tear her to pieces, Ahmed had sprang forward, seized a piece of iron, one end of which was red hot, from the shop of a blacksmith, and thrust it furiously into the face of the lion. With a cry of pain and rage the lion left the princess and bounded off to the bazaars, where he did great damage.

As soon as the princess had recovered from her fright, she beckoned to Ahmed to come near, and removing her veil, told him he was a brave little fellow, and ordered one of her servants to give him a purse of gold. Ahmed had never seen anyone so beautiful, and was so lost in wonder, that before he could find words of thanks, the party had passed on.

But when the money was spent, Ahmed and his father began to be in want again. A Jewish pedlar having told him how much better trade was in the capital, they determined to set forth to that city, though the way was long and full of danger. "Better to die in the desert, than in the heart of a great city," said Ahmed.

So they set forth on their journey, sometimes climbing up winding paths among the mountains, at other times traversing the desert, footsore, and weary almost to death, often hungry and thirsty, tormented by the thought that they would fall into the hands of the man-stealing robbers who haunted this great pilgrim road.

On account of the intense heat and the cruel robbers, they traveled by night. In every shadow cast by the moon upon the ground, they thought they saw a robber on his big horse. During the day they slept at wayside inns, and in return for little services rendered by Ahmed to the muleteers, they would give him a handful of rice or bread, or a few dried fruits which kept them from starvation.

So it went on until one night, when searching for the bridge that crosses the Salt River, the sky became suddenly overcast, the rain fell in torrents, and soon the river was in flood. There was nothing to be done but to sit down and wait until the moon should rise. The fierce wind buffeted them, the rain drenched them; they had lost their way, and were at the mercy of wild beasts.

Once, when the wind dropped for a little, out of the darkness came a groan. "Keep still as death, my son," said the father to Ahmed, "for it is the Old Man of the Desert."

Now Ahmed had never before heard of the Old Man of the Desert, and therefore knew no fear, so despite his father's warning, he got up and

went in the direction from whence came the groans. As he reached the spot, the moon came out from behind a bank of clouds, and Ahmed saw a poor dervish lying on the sand. He had a leopard skin thrown over his shoulders; by his side lay a big stick studded with sharp nails, and a basin made of the outer skin of a pumpkin in which he collected alms.

"For the sake of the Prophet," he moaned when he saw Ahmed, "give me a drink of water." And Ahmed, filling his pitcher from the river gave him to drink, though the water was somewhat salty.

The water revived the dervish, and he said: "I am Ali, the dervish, and am known throughout Persia. Two months ago I left Mazandaran to go to Meshed. But yesterday the fever seized me.

This is the third attack, and, as you know, it is always fatal.

"Stay with me, my son, in this dark hour when I shall pass through the valley of the shadow of death. And when my soul shall have crossed the Bridge of Death, take this little leather bag hanging round my neck, and therein you shall find a tiny cup, cut from a crystal, which if used rightly, shall lift thee to great power and wealth.

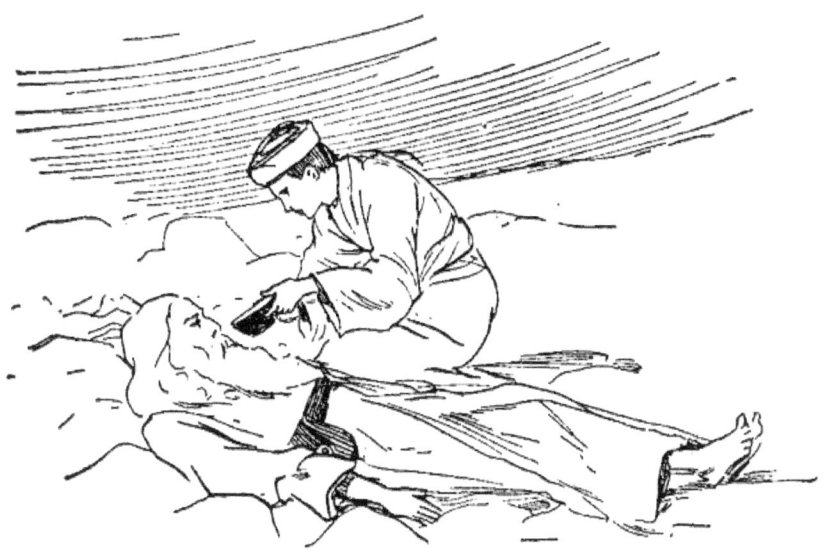

"Each morning when you rise, place a drop of pure water in the cup, and look intently therein, and should any danger threaten you or those near and dear to you, it will be made manifest. And if—" but here his strength failed him, his head fell back, and he passed away. Ahmed found the bag and the beautifully cut crystal, just as the dervish had said, and returning to his father, told him all that had happened.

Ahmed did as the dervish had directed him for several mornings, but seeing nothing in the crystal, he dropped the practice. There came a day, however, when they were overtaken by a dreadful dust storm. From across the wide stretch of sand, the wind raged, the sky and sun were blotted out, the air was laden with dust, and the small pebbles and stones carried in the wind cut them until they cried with pain. Shelter there was none.

In fear and pain they ran here and there, and when after several hours of misery, the storm had passed, they could not see each other. They were lost in the cruel desert, with no food, and worse still, no water. Sobbing in despair, Ahmed straggled on. He went like one in a dream. Time after time he fell tripping over rocks and bushes, but he pressed onward. Then came a time when he could go no further, and he lay down to die.

For a long time he slept, and then he was awakened by being shaken. Looking up, he saw an old man smiling and saying: "Why, it's little Ahmed, the son of Abdullah, the Soap Seller. Don't you know me, Ahmed? I am your uncle. Don't cry because you have lost your way. Come, take my hand and we will soon find your father."

Now Ahmed wondered why he had never seen or

even heard his father speak of this particular uncle, but he took the old man's hand, and together they set forth. Mile after mile they went, but no trace of his father could be found. Then he sat down crying, and said: "I am so tired, I can go no further." And the old man replied: "Sleep, my son, while I keep watch."

But just as Ahmed was closing his eyes, the old man turned, and Ahmed saw that he had thin legs like those of a sheep. "The Ghool! the Ghool!" he shrieked, and fainted. Then this wicked ogre of the desert began to open Ahmed's coat in order to suck his blood.

But another cry answered that of the boy, and then appeared on the scene a beautiful young

woman, carrying in her harid a necklace of gold
and silver beads. Casting but one glance at the
beads, the old man flew swifter than the wild
sheep of the mountains, for the sight of metal
rendered him powerless to do harm.

Of course, it was the princess whose life Ahmed
had saved in Meshed. The King, her father,
happened to be returning from a pilgrimage, and
to give a fright to her servants, she had
scampered off the track, and thus had found
Ahmed. At her request, Ahmed became one of
the King's followers, and together with his
father, whom they found the next day, they
journeyed to the capital.

Some three days' march from the capital, in the mountains near Kazveen, there lived the Old Man of the Mountains, or as he is generally known, the King of the Assassins, with his followers. So great was his power that he had but to say the word and any of his men would throw themselves from the topmost crags to the valleys beneath and be dashed to pieces, or at his bidding, they would travel forth to the most distant parts of the world in order to kill any persons, however great they might be.

When he heard that the King of Persia was collecting an army to destroy both him and his tribe, he became very angry, and said to one of his followers: "Go, rid me of the King of Persia;" and the mart-took bread and water and a sharp dagger, and went.

Now after his narrow escape from the Old Man of the Desert, Ahmed took pains every morning to place a drop of water in the crystal cup and look therein. Nothing appeared until one morning he saw in the bead of water a vision of the King asleep, and standing by him a robber with an uplifted dagger, about to strike. Hurrying to the King's presence, he warned him of the danger, but the King only laughed, for he trusted his guards.

Nevertheless, Ahmed determined to keep watch. Darkness came, and the guards slept. The palace was silent. The hours slipped by, and Ahmed,

weary with much waiting was about to retire, when he perceived a dark shadow creeping into that part of the palace where the King slept.

The figure noiselessly made its way to the very threshold of the King's room, when Ahmed sprang upon it, at the same time giving the alarm. The whole palace was aroused and the murdered secured.

When the messenger did not return, the Old Man of the Mountains sent a second, and then a third, and finally the most daring and skilful of all his followers; but thanks to Ahmed's crystal cup, all attempts upon the life of the King failed.

Then the King sent for Ahmed, and said: "Ask for anything in reason, and it shall be given thee." And though he was trembling in every limb, Ahmed replied: "Neither wealth nor power does thy slave desire, save the hand of thy daughter."

"If she loves you, it shall be so," replied the King, and she did love him; they were married, and Ahmed became the King's Prime Minister.

THE KING'S TREASURE

Accurately relating how a marked advance in material
and political prosperity accrued to Abdul Karim, and
the part played by a monarch whose philosophy
included the immediate advancement of
a worthy subject.

ALABORING man named Abdul Karim, with his
wife, Zeeba—"the beautiful one"—lived in a

sheltered valley, surrounded by hills, the sides of which were covered with fine gardens, in which the peach, the grape, the mulberry, and other delicious fruits grew in great profusion.

Although his wife's name was Zeeba, as a matter of fact, she was very plain in appearance. But from having been named Zeeba, she really thought she was beautiful, and thus it came about that, moved by vanity, her two children were named, the boy, Yusuf, or Joseph, who as you know, was sold by his brethren into Egypt and became next to the King; and the girl, Fatima, after Fatima, the favorite daughter of Mahomet, and the wife of the famous Ali.

Now Abdul Karim was only a laborer on the land, receiving no wages, merely being paid in grain and cloth sufficient for the wants of himself and family. Of money he knew nothing except by name.

One day his master was so pleased with his work that he actually gave him ten "krans," equivalent to about a dollar of our money. To Abdul Karim this seemed great wealth, and directly his day's work was done, he ran home to his wife and said: "Look, Zeeba, there's riches for you!" and spread out the money before her. His good wife was delighted, and so were the children.

Then Abdul Karim said: "How shall we spend this great sum? The master has also given me a

day's holiday, so if you don't mind, I will go to the famous city of Meshed, which is only twenty miles from here, and after placing two krans on the shrine of the holy Imam, I will then visit the bazaars and buy everything you and the children desire."

"You would better buy me a piece of silk for a new dress," said Zeeba.

"I want a fine horse and a sword," said little Yusuf.

"I would like an Indian handkerchief and a pair of gold slippers," said Fatima.

"They shall be here by to-morrow night," said the father, and taking a big stick, he set off on his journey.

When he had come down from the mountains to the plain below, Abdul Karim saw stretched

before him the glorious city, and was lost in wonder at the sight of the splendid domes, where roofs glittered with gold, and the minarets, from the tops of which the priests were calling the people to prayer.

Then coming to the gate of the shrine, he asked an old priest if he might enter. "Yes, my son," was the reply. "Go in and give what thou canst spare to the mosque, and Allah will reward thee."

So Abdul Karim walked through the great court, amidst worshipers from every city in Asia. With open-mouthed astonishment he gazed on the riches of the temple, the jewels, the lovely carpets, the silks, the golden ornaments, and with humility he placed his two pieces of money on the sacred tomb. Then through the noise and bustle of the crowded streets, he went until he found the bazaars.

He found the sellers of fruits in one place, in another those who sold pots and pans, then he came to the jewelers, the bakers, the butchers, each trade having its own part of the bazaar, and so on, until he reached that part where there were only those who sold silks.

He entered one of the shops and asked to see some silks, and after much picking and choosing, fixed upon a superb piece of purple silk with an embroidered border of exquisite design. "I will take this," he said. "What is the price?"

"I shall only ask you two hundred krans, as you are a new customer," said the shopkeeper. "Anybody else but you would have to pay three or four hundred."

"Two hundred krans," repeated Abdul Karim, in astonishment. "Surely you have made a mistake. Do you mean krans like these?" taking one out of his pocket.

"Certainly I do," replied the shopkeeper, "and let me tell you it is very cheap at that price."

Abdul Karim pictured the disappointment of his wife. "Poor Zeeba," he sighed.

"Poor who?" said the silk merchant.

"My wife," said Abdul Karim.

"What have I to do with your wife?" asked the merchant, getting angry because he saw that all his trouble was in vain.

"I will tell you about it," said Abdul Karim. "Because I did my work well, my master gave me ten krans, the first time I ever have had any money. After giving two krans to the shrine, I intended to buy a piece of silk for my wife, a horse and sword for my little boy Yusuf, and an Indian handkerchief and a pair of gold slippers for my little girl Fatima. And here you ask me two hundred krans for one piece of silk. How can I pay you and buy the other things?"

"Here I have been wasting my time and rumpling my beautiful silks for a fool like you," cried the angry merchant. "Get out of my shop! Go home to your stupid Zeeba and your stupid children. Buy them some stale cakes and some black sugar, and don't put your head in my shop again, or it will be worse for you."

Then he took off his slipper, and with many blows drove poor Abdul Karim out into the street. Then Abdul Karim went to the horse market, only to find that the lowest-priced horse would cost two hundred and fifty krans.

The horse dealer mocked him when they found he had only eight krans, and suggested that he buy the sixteenth part of a donkey for his little son. As for a sword, he found that it would cost at least thirty krans; while a pair of golden slippers would run into many hundreds of krans; and for an Indian handkerchief, the price was twelve krans.

As poor Abdul Karim bent his weary way home, he met a beggar crying: "Dear friend, give me something, for to-morrow is Friday"—the Mahommedan Sunday. "He that giveth to the poor, lendeth to the Lord, and of a certainty the Lord will pay him back a hundredfold."

"Of all the men I have met to-day, you are the only one with whom I can deal," said simple Abdul Karim. "Here are eight krans. Use them in the service of God, and don't forget to pay me back a hundredfold."

Wrapping up the eight krans very carefully, the cunning beggar promised some day to return them a hundredfold.

At last Abdul Karim came in sight of his cottage, and little Yusuf, who had been all day on the look-out for him, ran breathlessly to meet him. "Where's my horse and sword, father?" he cried. And Fatima, who had just come up, called out, "And my handkerchief and golden slippers?" And Zeeba asked for her bit of silk.

Poor Abdul Karim looked so confused, that his wife said: "Be quiet, my dears. Your father could not bring them all with him, so he has packed them on Yusuf's horse and left him in charge of a servant, who will be here presently." But when she heard his story, and above all that he had given eight krans to a beggar, she got very angry, and marched off and told the master.

But the master was still more angry, and said: "What! the blockhead gave his eight krans to a beggar? Send him to me." And when Abdul Karim came before him, he said scornfully: "You must fancy yourself a big man, Abdul. I never give more than a copper coin to a beggar, but your Excellency gives them silver. The beggar promised that you should be repaid a hundredfold, did he? And it shall be so, even now." Then as Abdul's face brightened, he laughed and said: "Not in money, but in stripes." And his servants threw Abdul on the ground and gave him one hundred blows on his bare feet.

The next day, Abdul's master sent for him again, and after calling him a fool, said: "I have a nice little job for you, that will bring you to your proper senses. Go into the field and dig for water, day after day until you find it."

So for many days Abdul labored under the scorching sun, until he had dug down to a depth of about thirty feet, and then he came upon a brass vessel, finely chased, full of round white stones, which fairly dazzled his eyes in the fierce sunlight. He put one in his mouth and tried to break it with his teeth, but could not.

Then he said to himself, "The master has planted some rice and it has turned into stones. Perhaps there are some more." And going down a few feet lower, he found another pot filled with sparkling stones of various colors.

Then he remembered that he had seen pretty pieces of glass like these for sale in Meshed, and made up his mind that on the first opportunity he would again visit the city and take the stones with him. Meanwhile, he would hide them, and say nothing.

Abdul did not have to wait long for a holiday, for on finding water a little lower down, his master was so pleased that he gave him a well- deserved rest, and then Abdul set off for Meshed. But before entering the city, he hid most of the treasure at the foot of a tree under a big stone. Then with still a pocket full, he went straight to the shop where he had seen such stones, and spoke to the shopkeeper who was seated at the entrance to his shop, calmly smoking his water-pipe.

"Do you want to buy any more stones like those?" he asked, pointing to some in a brass tray. "Yes, have you got one?" replied the merchant, for Abdul did not look like a man who was likely to have more than one, if any.

"I have a pocket full of them," said Abdul.

"You have a pocket full of pebbles, more likely,"

said the jeweler. But when Abdul took out a handful and showed him, he was so astonished that he could hardly speak. Trembling in every limb, he bade Abdul wait a minute, and leaving his apprentice in charge, he hastily left the shop. When he returned, the chief of the police was with him.

"I am innocent," cried the jeweler. "There is the man. His pockets are filled with diamonds, rubies, emeralds, and pearls of great price. Without doubt he has found the long-lost treasure of Cyrus."

Then Abdul was searched; the precious stones were found upon him; and when they had brought Zeeba and the children, the whole family were sent under a guard of five hundred soldiers to the capital.

While all these things were taking place, the King saw in his dreams, for three nights, one after the other, the Holy Prophet, who, looking steadfastly at him, exclaimed: "Abbas, protect and favor my friend." And on the third night, the King took courage and said to the Prophet: "And who is thy friend?" And the answer came:

"He is a poor laboring man, Abdul Karim by name, who of his poverty gave one-fifth to the shrine at Meshed, and now, because he has found the King's treasure, they have bound him, and are bringing him to this city to oppress him."

So the King went forth two days' journey to meet Abdul. First came one hundred horsemen. Next, poor Abdul, seated on a camel, with his arms bound tightly. Walking behind the camel were the weeping children and their mother. Then came the foot soldiers guarding the treasure. The King made the camel kneel down, and with his own hands undid the cruel bonds.

Then with tears running down his face, Abdul knelt before the King and pleaded for his dear ones, saying: "If thou slay me, at least let these innocent ones go free!"

Lifting Abdul from the ground, the King then said: "I am come to honor, not to slay thee. When thou hast rested, thou shalt return to thine own province, not as a prisoner, but as the Governor thereof." And smiling, he added:

"Already is the silk dress prepared for Zeeba; the horse and sword for Yusuf; and the Indian handkerchief and the golden slippers for Fatima have not been forgotten." For the King had read in the report of the chief of police all the details of Abdul's case.

And so it was that Abdul's piety and gift to the shrine had come back, not a hundredfold, but beyond his wildest dreams, and the shrine and the poor benefited greatly thereby.

The King and the Fisherman

Illustrating the advantage of being able to formulate
a judicious reply to an embarrassing question,
especially when material plenitude
may ensue.

THE countries washed by the great rivers Tigris
and Euphrates were once ruled by a certain King
who was passionately fond of fish.

He was seated one day with Sherem, his wife, in
the royal gardens that stretch down to the banks
of the Tigris, at the point where it is spanned by
the wonderful bridge of boats; and looking up
spied a boat gliding by, in which was seated a
fisherman having a large fish.

Noticing that the King was looking closely at
him, and knowing how much the King liked this
particular kind of fish, the fisherman made his
obeisance, and skilfully bringing his boat to the
shore, came before the King and begged that he
would accept the fish as a present. The King was
greatly pleased at this, and ordered that a large
sum of money be given to the fisherman.

But before the fisherman had left the royal presence, the Queen turned towards the King and said: "You have done a foolish thing." The King was astonished to hear her speak in this way, and asked how that could be. The Queen replied:

"The news of your having given so large a reward for so small a gift will spread through the city and it will be known as the fisherman's gift. Every fisherman who catches a big fish will bring it to the palace, and should he not be paid in like manner, he will go away discontented, and secretly speak evil of you among his fellows."

"Thou speakest the truth, light of my eyes," said the King, "but can not you see how mean it would be for a King, if for that reason he were to take back his gift?" Then perceiving that the Queen was ready to argue the matter, he turned away angrily, saying: "The matter is closed."

However, later in the day, when he was in a more amiable frame of mind, the Queen again approached him, and said that if that was his only reason for not taking back his gift, she would arrange it. "You must summon the fisherman," she said, "and then ask him, 'Is this fish male or female?' If he says male, then you will tell him that you wanted a female fish; but if he should say female, your reply will be that you wanted a male fish. In this way the matter will be properly adjusted."

The King thought this an easy way out of the difficulty, and commanded the fisherman to be brought before him. When the fisherman, who by the way, was a most intelligent man, stood before the King, the King said to him: "O fisherman, tell me, is this fish male or female?"

The fisherman replied, "The fish is neither male nor female." Whereupon the King smiled at the clever answer, and to add to the Queen's annoyance, directed the keeper of the royal purse to give the fisherman a further sum of money.

Then the fisherman placed the money in his leather bag, thanked the King, and swinging the bag over his shoulder, hurried away, but not so quickly that he did not notice that he had dropped one small coin. Placing the bag on the ground, he stooped and picked up the coin, and again went on his way, with the King and Queen carefully watching his every action.

"Look! what a miser he is!" said Sherem, triumphantly. "He actually put down his bag to pick up one small coin because it grieved him to think that it might reach the hands of one of the King's servants, or some poor person, who, needing it, would buy bread and pray for the long life of the King."

"Again thou speakest the truth," replied the King, feeling the justice of this remark; and once more was the fisherman brought into the royal presence. "Are you a human being or a beast?" the King asked him. "Although I made it possible for you to become rich without toil, yet the miser within you could not allow you to leave even one small piece of money for others." Then the King bade him to go forth and show his face no more within the city.

At this the fisherman fell on his knees and cried: "Hear me, O King, protector of the poor! May God grant the King a long life. Not for its value did thy servant pick up the coin, but because on one side it bore the name of God, and on the other the likeness of the King. Thy servant feared that someone, not seeing the coin, would tread it into the dirt, and thus defile both the name of God and the face of the King. Let the King judge if by so doing I have merited reproach."

This answer pleased the King beyond all measure, and he gave the fisherman another large sum of money. And the Queen's wrath was turned away, and she looked kindly upon the fisherman as he departed with his bag laden with money.